# It's Not Fair!

First published in 2010
by Wayland

Text copyright © Jillian Powell
Illustration copyright © Mark Chambers

Wayland
338 Euston Road
London NW1 3BH

Wayland Australia
Level 17/207 Kent Street
Sydney, NSW 2000

Series Editor: Louise John
Cover design: Paul Cherrill
Design: D.R.ink
Consultant: Shirley Bickler

A CIP catalogue record for this book is available from the British Library.

ISBN 9780750261975

Printed in China

Wayland is a division of Hachette Children's Books,
an Hachette UK Company

www.hachette.co.uk

# It's Not Fair!

Written by Jillian Powell
Illustrated by Mark Chambers

WAYLAND

Tilly was on holiday, but she had a broken arm.

"Look, bikes!" said Dad.

"I can't go on a bike!"
said Tilly.

"Look at the swimming pool," said Todd. "It has a slide!"

"Oh, dear. I can't go swimming," said Tilly.

"Bowling?" said Dad.

10

"No," said Tilly. "I can't go bowling."

"I know! We can play tennis," said Todd.

"But I can't play tennis!"
said Tilly.

"Look over there!" said Mum. "Crazy golf!"

"How can I play that?"
said Tilly.

"Let's just play ball,"
said Todd.

"But I can't do that!"
said Tilly.

Tilly sat down. She felt very cross.

"It's not fair!" she said.

"Come on, Tilly!" said
Todd. "I have an idea."

"A pedalo!" said Tilly.

"We can all do this," said
Todd. "Get pedalling, Tilly!"

**START READING** is a series of highly enjoyable books for beginner readers. **The books have been carefully graded to match the Book Bands widely used in schools.** This enables readers to be sure they choose books that match their own reading ability.

## Look out for the Band colour on the book in our Start Reading logo.

The Bands are:

Pink Band 1A & 1B

Red Band 2

Yellow Band 3

Green Band 5

Orange Band 6

Turquoise Band 7

Purple Band 8

Gold Band 9

**START READING** books can be read independently or shared with an adult. They promote the enjoyment of reading through satisfying stories supported by fun illustrations.

**Jillian Powell** began writing stories when she was four years old. She lives in a house beside a village church and sits down to write every day. She has written stories and rhymes about dogs, cats, scarecrows and crocodiles as well as children such as Tilly and Todd.

**Mark Chambers** lives in Lincoln. His studio, where he illustrates, is full of books, drawings and posters and is home to a lobster called Larry!